SIPPING SPIDERS THROUGH A STRAW

CAMPFIRE SONGS FOR MONSTERS

Lyrics by **Kelly DiPucchio**

Pictures by **Gris Grimly**

SCHOLASTIC PRESS | NEW YORK

Library of Congress Cataloging-in-Publication Data

DiPucchio, Kelly S.
Sipping spiders through a straw : campfire songs for monsters / verses by Kelly DiPucchio ; illustrations by Gris Grimly. - 1st ed.
v. cm.
Contents: A-camping we will go - Home of the strange - Sipping spiders through a straw - 99 bottles of blood on the wall - Harry
Finnigan - Take me out to the graveyard - Zombie Midge - For he's a stinky old fellow - My body lies over the ocean - My delicious
Frankenstein - Creepy, creepy little jar - Do your guts hang low? - I've been running over road toads - Little Big Foot's boo boo
- If you're scary and you know it - Where, oh where has my little frog gone - Slither and slink.
ISBN-13: 978-0-439-58401-2 (hardcover : alk. paper)
ISBN-10: 0-439-58401-9
1. Children's songs, English - Texts. [1. Camps - Songs and music. 2. Monsters - Songs and music. 3. Humorous songs.
4. Songs.] I. Grimly, Gris, ill. II. Title.

PZ8.3.D5998Sip 2008
[782.42]-dc22

2007000847

10 9 8 7 6 5 4 3 2 1   08 09 10 11 12
Printed in Singapore   46
First edition, May 2008

The text type was set in Latino-Rumba.
The display type was set in House of Terror.
The illustrations were done in watercolor and mixed media.

PLAYLIST

A-Camping We Will Go

Home of the Strange

Sipping Spiders Through a Straw

99 Bottles of Blood on the Wall

Blow, Blow, Blow Your Nose!

Harry Finnigan

My Delicious Frankenstein

Take Me Out to the Graveyard

Zombie Midge

For He's a Stinky Old Fellow

My Body Lies Over the Ocean

Creepy, Creepy Little Jar

Do Your Guts Hang Low?

I've Been Running Over Road Toads

Little Big Foot's Boo-Boo

If You're Scary and You Know It, Clap Your Paws

Where, Oh Where Has My Little Frog Gone?

Slither & Slink

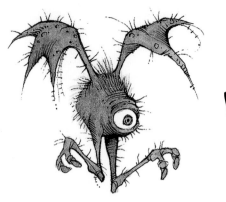

A-CAMPING
WE WILL GO

(SHRIEKED TO THE TUNE OF "THE FARMER IN THE DELL")

A-camping we will go,
with monster friends in tow—
Hi ho the scary-O,
we dare you to say no.
We'll gather 'round the pit.
We'll growl, snort, and spit.
Hi ho the scary-O,
now grab a log and sit.
We'll sing a song or two.
We'll belch and barbecue.
Hi ho the scary-O,
here, try the witches' brew.
We'll rip your tent and sneer.
We'll fill your nights with fear.
Hi ho the scary-O,
we're glad you made it here.

HOME of the STRANGE

(GRUNTED TO THE TUNE OF "HOME ON THE RANGE")

Oh, give me a home

where the Boogie Men roam,

where the ghosts and the green goblins play.

Where there aren't any phones,

only grunts, shrieks, and moans

and the flies are all welcome to stay.

Home, home of the strange,

where the feared and the freaks come to play.

Where the stench in the air,

comes from goon underwear

and the kids are all pasty and gray.

SIPPING SPIDERS
THROUGH A STRAW

(BURPED TO THE TUNE OF "SIPPING CIDER THROUGH A STRAW")

The biggest fly
The biggest fly

I ever saw
I ever saw

was sipping spiders
was sipping spiders

right through a straw.
right through a straw.

I asked him if
I asked him if

he'd show me how
he'd show me how

to sip those spiders
to sip those spiders

and share his chow.
and share his chow.

Then wart to wing
Then wart to wing

and eye to jaw
and eye to jaw

we sipped those spiders
we sipped those spiders

right through a straw.
right through a straw.

From time to time
From time to time

that straw would slip
that straw would slip

and we'd sip spiders
and we'd sip spiders

fly trap to lip.
fly trap to lip.

And now I have
And now I have

a fly-in-law
a fly-in-law

and lots of maggots
and lots of maggots

to call me Ma.
to call me Ma.

I'll tell you this
I'll tell you this

before you try,
before you try,

don't sip your spiders...

... JUST EAT THE FLY!

99 BOTTLES OF BLOOD ON THE WALL

99 bottles of blood on the wall.

99 bottles of blood.

Take a big slurp,

and let out a burp . . .

. . . 98 BOTTLES OF BLOOD ON THE WALL.

BLOW, BLOW, BLOW YOUR NOSE!

(SNIVELED TO THE TUNE OF "ROW, ROW, ROW YOUR BOAT")

Blow, blow, blow your nose
  sick and stuffy ghost.
    Pick it,
      and poke it,
        and pull it out,
          and spread it on your toast.

HARRY FINNIGAN

(HOWLED TO THE TUNE OF "MICHAEL FINNIGAN")

There was a young boy named Harry Finnigan.

He grew whiskers on his chinnigin.

The moon came out, his hair grew inagin.

Howlin' hairy Harry Finnigan.

There was a young boy named Harry Finnigan.

He smoothed hair gel on his face and feetagin.

Broke ten combs then shaved his backagin.

Messy, hairy Harry Finnigan.

There was a young boy named Harry Finnigan.

He played with wolves then hurried homeagin.

The sun came up, his fur fell outagin…

…now he's naked Harry Finnigan.

MY DELICIOUS FRANKENSTEIN

(SCREAMED TO THE TUNE OF "OH, MY DARLING CLEMENTINE")

In a kitchen, in a castle,

filled with mold and turpentine,

lived a baker, monster maker,

and her true love, Frankenstein.

Oh, my crispy. Oh, my crunchy.

Oh, my frosted Frankenstein.

You're so yummy... in my tummy...

My delicious Frankenstein.

TAKE ME OUT to the GRAVEYARD

(CHATTERED TO THE TUNE OF "TAKE ME OUT TO THE BALL GAME")

Take me out to the graveyard.

Take me out to the tombs.

Buy me some worms from that Quasi named Jack.

I don't care 'bout that hump on his back.

So it's boo, boo, boo, at the Bone team.

If they don't win then they're lame.

For it's one, two, three bites you're out

at the graveyard game!

ZOMBIE MIDGE

(MOANED TO THE TUNE OF "LONDON BRIDGE IS FALLING DOWN")

Zombie Midge is falling down,
rolling 'round, all through town.
Zombie Midge is falling down.
My pale lady.
Lift her with a walking cane,
a reel and chain, a giant crane.
Lift her with Kong's little plane.
My stale lady.

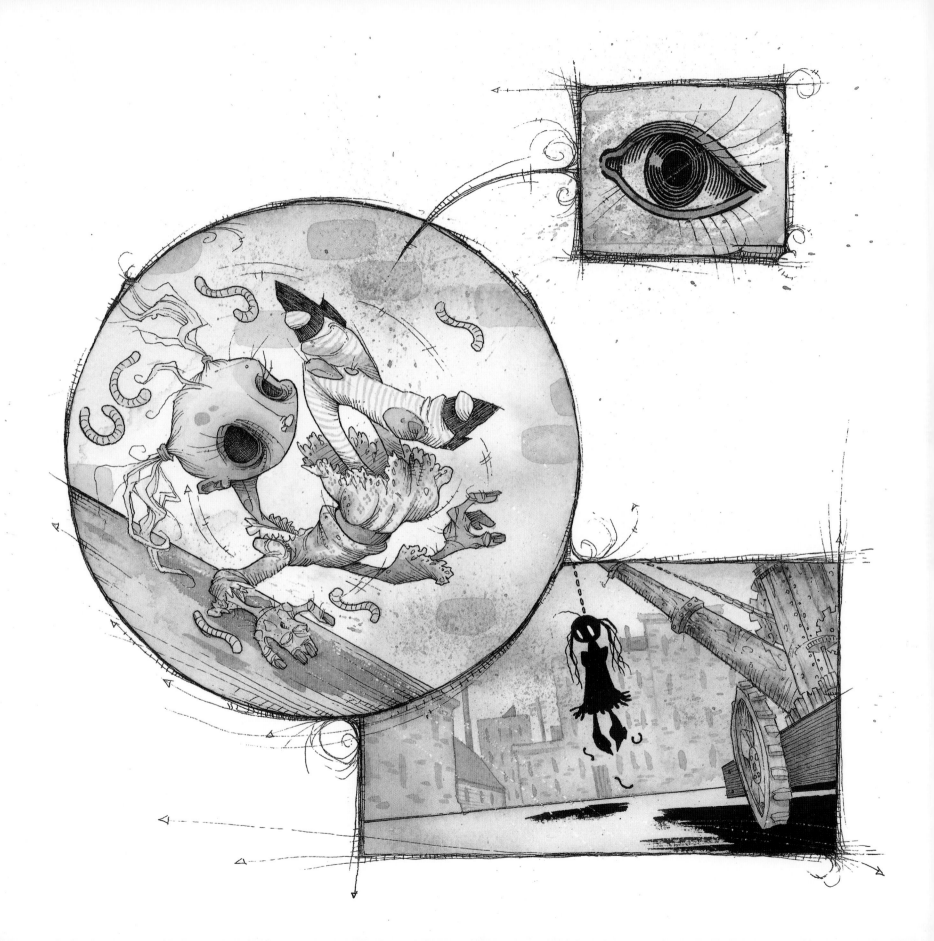

FOR HE'S A
STINKY OLD FELLOW

(SNARLED TO THE TUNE OF "FOR HE'S A JOLLY GOOD FELLOW")

For he's a stinky old fellow.
He's got teeth that are yellow.
He reeks of a horrible smell-o...
One whiff of his breath and you'll die!

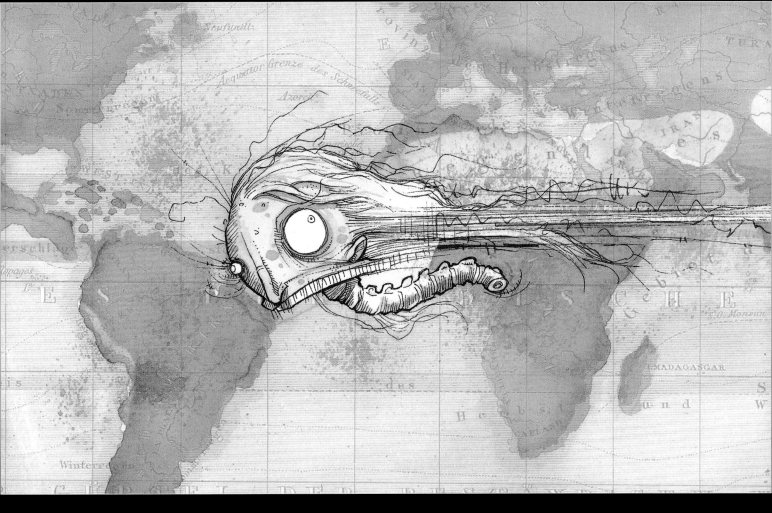

MY BODY LIES
OVER THE OCEAN

(SOBBED TO THE TUNE OF "MY BONNIE LIES OVER THE OCEAN")

My body lies over the ocean.

My body lies over the sea.

My body lies over the ocean.

Oh, bring back my body to me!

CREEPY, CREEPY LITTLE JAR

(WHISPERED TO THE TUNE OF "TWINKLE, TWINKLE, LITTLE STAR")

Creepy, creepy little jar,
how I wonder what you are.
Up upon that shelf so high,
like a pickled, shriveled guy.
Creepy, creepy little jar—
You can stay just where you are.

DO YOUR GUTS HANG LOW?

(SCREECHED TO THE TUNE OF "DO YOUR EARS HANG LOW?")

Do your guts hang low?

Do they wobble to and fro?

Can you tie them in a knot?

Can you feed them to a crow?

Can you jump rope with your mother?

Can you tie up your big brother?

Do your guts hang low?

I'VE BEEN
RUNNING OVER
ROAD TOADS

(CROAKED TO THE TUNE OF "I'VE BEEN WORKING ON THE RAILROAD")

I've been running over road toads

all the livelong day.

I've been running over road toads,

"Just hurry, hop away!"

Can't you hear me loudly honking?

I must've hit nine or ten.

Can't you hear my frantic shouting…?

Oops, I did it again!

LITTLE BIG FOOT'S Boo-Boo

(GROWLED TO THE TUNE OF "LITTLE BUNNY FOO FOO")

Big Foot got a boo-boo
running through the forest.
He landed on a city street
and bumped his furry head.
Along came Mama Hairy, and this is what she said:

"I'm sorry 'bout your boo-boo,
but I don't want to see you
wandering those city streets,
you'll end up in the zoo-zoo!"

IF YOU'RE SCARY AND YOU KNOW IT,
CLAP YOUR PAWS

(ROARED TO THE TUNE OF "IF YOU'RE HAPPY AND YOU KNOW IT")

If you're scary and you know it, clap your paws.

If you're scary and you know it, flap your jaws.

If you're scary and you know it, and you really want to show it,

if you're scary and you know it, snap your claws.

WHERE, OH WHERE HAS MY LITTLE FROG GONE?

(CACKLED TO THE TUNE OF "OH WHERE HAS MY LITTLE DOG GONE?")

Where, oh where has my little frog gone?

Oh where, oh where can he be?

With his warts so big and his tongue so long,

he is so precious to me!

Where, oh where has my little frog gone?

Oh what, oh what shall I do?

I need my little frog home with me now

so I can finish my brew!

SLITHER & SLINK

(HISSED TO THE TUNE OF "SKINNAMARINK")

Slither and slink and stink and wink
Slither and stinky-doooo—
We... scare... you!
We scare you in the basement
and in the garden shed.
We scare you in your closet
and underneath the bed...
Oh...
Slither and slink and stink and wink
Slither and stinky-doooo—
Bye-bye — BOO!
We really scare you!
Bye-bye — BOO!